A *New York Times* Bestseller

A Junior Library Guild Selection

An American Library Association
Notable Children's Book Nominee

Two for One

- -

★ "It would be no surprise if Bink and Gollie were to join the likes of
Elephant and Piggie and Frog and Toad in the ranks of favorite friend
duos." — *School Library Journal* (starred review)

★ "B&G again hit that sweet spot where picture books, graphic novels, and
early readers converge . . . and readers will be as delighted as Bink and
Gollie about the fortuneteller-certified long-term soundness of their
friendship." — *Bulletin of the Center for Children's Books* (starred review)

"Utterly chuckle-worthy, charming, and (thank goodness) still refreshing.
Friendships can be tricky to navigate, but if youngsters find half of the
joy and loyalty of this pair, they'll be set." — *Kirkus Reviews*

BINK & gollie

Two for One

Kate DiCamillo and Alison McGhee

illustrated by Tony Fucile

CANDLEWICK PRESS

For Janie, a blue-ribbon friend

K. D.

To Caroly Bintz

A. M.

To Elinor and Eli, great buddies of mine

T. F.

First paperback edition 2013

Library of Congress Cataloging-in-Publication Data for the hardcover edition is available.

Library of Congress Catalog Card Number 2011046625

ISBN 978-0-7636-3361-5 (hardcover)

ISBN 978-0-7636-6445-9 (paperback)

14 15 16 17 18 SCP 10 9 8 7 6 5 4 3

Printed in Humen, Dongguan, China

This book was typeset in Humana Sans.
The illustrations were done digitally.

Candlewick Press
99 Dover Street
Somerville, Massachusetts 02144

visit us at www.candlewick.com

Contents

"Gollie, do you think we should go to the state fair?"

Whack

a

Duck

"I'm going to whack a duck," said Bink.

"Step right up," said the duck man. "Whack a duck!"

"I'm going to win the world's largest donut," said Bink.

"Of course you are, little lady," said the Whack-a-Duck man. "You've got *winner* written all over you."

"I do?" said Bink.

"She does?" said Gollie.

"What a happy, happy day," said the duck man. "How I love it when little ladies win large donuts."

"She hasn't won it yet," said Gollie.

"Who doesn't love a donut?" said the duck man. "Who doesn't love a large donut? Donuts are nature's most perfect food."

"They are?" said Gollie.

"Did I win?" said Bink.

"I don't think so," said Gollie.

11

"Step right up," said the duck man.
"Whack a donut! Win a duck."

"Uh-oh," said Gollie.

"Did I win?" said Bink.

"Whack something?" said the duck man.
"Win something?"

"I fear this can only end in tragedy," said Gollie.

"Did I win?" said Bink.

"Oh, Bink," said Gollie. "There are no winners here."

"Don't worry, Bink," said Gollie. "I'm sure the
Whack-a-Duck man will be just fine."

"But I've never seen a grown man cry before,"
said Bink.

"Three bags of donuts, please," said Bink.

"I didn't win," said Bink.

"But we're all still alive," said Gollie.

"Duck a whack," said the duck man. "Step right up."

You're
Special,
Aren't
You?

"Oh, Bink," said Gollie. "How I would love to be in a talent show."

"But you have to stand on a stage,"
said Bink.

"I can do that," said Gollie.

"But you have to stand on a stage in
front of an audience," said Bink.

"I can do that," said Gollie.

"All righty, then," said Bink.

"Pardon me," said Gollie. "Are you in charge
  of the talent show?"

"Do you have a talent?" said the judge.

"I do," said Gollie. "In fact, I have several."

"That there is a top-quality talent," said the judge.

"Uh-oh," said Bink.

"Incoming!" said the judge.

"I can't even guess," said the judge.

"That's my friend," said Bink.

"What's her talent?" said the judge.

"She has several," said Bink.

"What did you say her talent was again?"
said the judge.

"Here it comes," said Bink. "Here comes
Gollie's talent."

43

"You call that talent?" said the judge.

"Gollie!" said Bink.

"Gollie," said Bink, "were you afraid up there?"

"Yes," said Gollie.

"What was your talent?" said Bink.

"I was going to recite a poem," said Gollie. "Onstage. In front of an audience."

"These cows are listening," said Bink.
"And so am I."

"'Old MacDonald,'" said Gollie.

"Oh!" said Bink. "I know that one!"

" 'Had a farm,' " said Gollie. " 'E, I.' "

" 'E, I,' " said Bink.

" 'O,' " said Bink and Gollie together.

Without
Question

"I love my chipmunk balloon," said Bink.

"I love my scepter and crown," said Gollie.

"What's next?" said Bink. "The Ferris wheel? The Big Daddy Octopus? The Bump-a-Rama bumper cars?"

"Destiny," said Gollie.

"Destiny?" said Bink. "Is it a ride?"

"In a manner of speaking," said Gollie.

"Girls," said Madame Prunely, "come inside."

"Welcome, all you who travel on the darkened path," said Madame Prunely.

"Are we traveling on a darkened path?" said Bink.

"Shhh," said Gollie.

"I gaze into my crystal ball," said Madame Prunely.

"Can I look, too?" said Bink.

"I gaze into my crystal ball," said Madame Prunely. "And I see that the past is replete with loss. A donut. A duck. Talent without applause."

"She's right, Gollie," said Bink. "There was a donut. There was a duck."

"And no one clapped for me," said Gollie.

"Talk about a darkened path," said Bink.

"But enough about the past," said Madame
Prunely. "Let us take a look at the future."

"I see two friends," said Madame Prunely.

"Is one of those friends tall?" said Gollie.

"Yes," said Madame Prunely.

"And is the other friend short?" said Bink.

"Yes," said Madame Prunely.

"Are they together?" said Gollie.

"Without question," said Madame Prunely.

About the Creators

Kate DiCamillo is the author of *The Magician's Elephant*, a *New York Times* bestseller; *The Tale of Despereaux*, which was awarded the Newbery Medal; *Because of Winn-Dixie*, a Newbery Honor Book; and six books starring Mercy Watson, including the Theodor Seuss Geisel Honor Book *Mercy Watson Goes for a Ride*. She lives in Minneapolis.

Alison McGhee is the author of several picture books, including *Song of Middle C*, illustrated by Scott Menchin, and the #1 *New York Times* bestseller *Someday*, illustrated by Peter H. Reynolds; novels for children and young adults, including *All Rivers Flow to the Sea* and the Julia Gillian series; and several novels for adults, including the best-selling *Shadow Baby*, which was a *Today* Book Club selection and was nominated for a Pulitzer Prize. She lives in Minnesota and Vermont.

Tony Fucile is the author-illustrator of *Let's Do Nothing!* and the illustrator of *Mitchell's License* by Hallie Durand. He has spent more than twenty years designing and animating characters for numerous feature films, including *The Lion King*, *Finding Nemo*, and *The Incredibles*. He lives in the San Francisco Bay area.

To learn more about the series and its creators,
visit www.binkandgollie.com.

Don't miss the book that started it all!

A *New York Times Book Review* Best Illustrated Children's Book of the Year

A Theodor Seuss Geisel Award Winner

An American Library Association Notable Children's Book

★ "More, please!" —*Kirkus Reviews* (starred review)

★ "Think Pippi Longstocking meets *The Big Bang Theory*."
— *Publishers Weekly* (starred review)

• • •

And look out for the third and final installment!

★ "The fresh, wry dialogue and Fucile's witty cartooning are as dynamic a pairing as Bink and Gollie themselves."
— *Publishers Weekly* (starred review)